BILLY HAS A BIRTHDAY

James Minter

Helen Rushworth – Illustrator

www.thebillybooks.co.uk

MINTER PUBLISHING LIMITED

Minter Publishing Limited (MPL)
4 Lauradale
Bracknell RG12 7DT

Copyright © James Minter 2014, 2015

Previously published as *Billy's Tenth Birthday,* 2014

James Minter has asserted his rights under the
Copyright, Design and Patents Act, 1988
to be the author of this work

Print ISBN: 978-1-910727-05-8

Illustrations copyright © Helen Rushworth

This book is sold subject to the condition that it shall not, by way of trade or otherwise, be lent, resold, hired out, or otherwise circulated in any form of binding or cover other than that in which it is published and without a similar condition, including this condition, being imposed on the subsequent purchaser.

<<<<<<

To those who think bullying and aggression are the way to go through life; you are so wrong.

<<<<<<

1

TEN, TEN, TEN

Turning ten years old, on the tenth day of the tenth month must be magical. Billy clapped his hands in excitement. Jacko, Billy's loving golden retriever dog, lay on the floor beside his bed.

'Ten, ten, ten, Jacko!' Billy said.

Billy often spoke to his dog about his feelings and thoughts.

'It's only seven days until my birthday!'

Jacko didn't seem to share Billy's excitement, and continued licking his paw.

'Turning ten is special; it's never going to

happen again … ever!' Billy ruffled the dog's fur. 'Are you listening to me?'

Jacko looked at Billy and licked his hand as if to say, *I'm hearing every word.*

'Do you know what, Jacko? I can count to over a thousand and spell marmalade.'

The golden retriever did not look impressed.

'I have learned so much, and can do all sorts of things, and I'm only nine. What's it going to be like when I'm ten?'

That reminded Billy of his best friend, Ant.

'Hey Jacko, you know Ant?'

Jacko wagged his tail upon hearing Ant's name.

'He can't spell London. I can. Everyone

but everyone knows there are two *'on's* in London and no *'no's*. Even Ant's little sister Max knows that, and she's only eight!'

'I hope Max can make it to my party. Mum said she won't count her as one of my six friends, which I am really pleased about. It's hard choosing who to invite to your party; somebody always gets left out.'

Thinking of his party got Billy wondering about birthday presents.

'I really hope that Mum and Dad are going to buy me a big bike so I can ride even faster than I already do. The trouble is that when other people buy you things they don't often get it right. It's not because they don't try or care, but more because I'm not exactly sure what I want. Seeing something on TV or on the Internet and actually holding it in your hands, are very different things.'

'I upset Mum last year by asking Grandad for money. She says I should be grateful for whatever I'm given. Mum is right, but Grandad never knows what to buy me. I think being nearly ten is old enough to ask for money, don't you?'

Jacko lifted his head and grasped Billy's pyjama bottoms with his teeth. He pulled.

Billy looked down at him. 'You're easy to buy for—a big bone and you're happy for hours. Asking for money isn't so bad. Actually, come to think of it, Grandad looked pleased the last time I asked for money. Toy shops and department stores aren't really his thing.'

Jacko was not listening; he was busy

tugging on Billy's pyjamas. He wanted to go outside for a walk.

'We'll walk later, Jacko,' Billy said, tugging back until Jacko let go. The dog slumped down and rested his head between his paws. He looked sad.

Feeling bad, Billy jumped out of bed, 'Come on then Jacko, let's go for a walk now!'

2

THE DAY OF BILLY'S BIRTHDAY

The Saturday of Billy's birthday finally arrived. His alarm woke him at seven o'clock. He wasn't going to miss the postman or give Jacko the chance to eat any of his cards.

Hearing the clink-clank sound of the letterbox, Billy threw his *Transformers* duvet to the floor, grabbed his red-and-white stripy dressing gown, and jumped into his slippers. He made a running, stumbling descent down the stairs.

Unhurt and full of excitement, Billy rugby-tackled Jacko, who was racing down the hall towards the letterbox. A six-stone golden retriever, travelling at full speed, takes some serious holding back. Billy, now ten years old, managed to find the extra strength to match his double-digit age.

He restrained the dog before anything was sniffed, chewed, slobbered on, or swung violently in a frenzied act of destruction. Instead of being annoyed, Jacko turned and gave Billy a good licking, followed by a beating from his excited wagging tail.

Billy shuffled through the post. Seeing his name, he picked out an envelope.

'Look, Jacko, this is mine! The one marked "Master W. Field."' Billy's real name was William but everyone called him Billy. Although his dad's name was Walter, and they shared the same initial, the envelope was addressed to 'Master W. Field', and not 'Mr W. Field'.

Billy knew the card was from his grandad. Although he lived only two streets away and very close to Ant, Grandad had posted it. Receiving letters in the post is always really exciting; that's what makes Grandad so special. Billy found three more envelopes addressed to him; one just had "Billy" scribbled across it in big blue felt-tip marker. *That must be from Ant,* he thought, *but he's never up this early, even on a school day! He must have asked his dad to deliver it on his way to work.*

Billy laid the four unopened cards on the

breakfast table. Then he sorted and stacked them in order, the top one to be opened first, saving the best for last. Grandad always chose great cards and he was Billy's only grandfather making his card doubly special. On top was Ant's card. He always wrote a joke inside, and this time was no different.

'What goes up but never comes down, Jacko?'

Billy tossed the card to one side, 'Everyone knows that. It's your age!'

The next two cards in the pile were from Billy's twin aunts.

'Look at these two, Jacko. My aunts might be twins, but they were born on different days and in different months. Auntie May was born on the 31st of May, just before midnight, and Auntie June was born thirty minutes later on the first day of June. How crazy is that? It's almost as crazy as me turning ten, on the tenth day of the tenth month!' Billy leapt around repeating the number over and over in disbelief that he had finally reached his double-digit birthday.

Sitting back down Billy fished out a gift voucher from each of his aunt's envelopes. 'Mum says it's because they live in Devon and it costs too much to send a present from there. Mum thinks that's a cop-out.' *Why don't they just send one card and one gift voucher? It would be a lot cheaper*, Billy thought.

Jacko rested his head on Billy's lap. He sniffed at the cards.

'Can you smell cats?' He brought the cards nearer to Jacko's nose. 'My aunts share their house with fourteen cats at the last count.'

Pouring milk over his Rice Krispies, Billy picked up his grandad's card and held it towards the light, hoping to get a hint of the contents. *Money, money, money* went through his mind.

'Please let it be money,' he begged. Milk dribbled down his chin as he took a spoonful of cereal, but with a quick wipe it was gone. Dressing gown sleeves were designed for such emergencies.

He grabbed the breadknife. Holding the blade away from him, he inched it along the envelope's seal. He didn't want to damage the money inside. Peering into the slit, he could make out a cartoon drawing. He pulled out the card, and saw it was a picture of a boy on a bicycle, wobbling along a potholed track. Expectation travelled down his spine.

As the card split apart no money fell out. 'Oh, Jacko.' His heart sank. 'I knew it.'

Confused and disappointed, he dropped the card and ran to his bedroom. He had been so sure his grandad had understood how important it was to him to get money. His eyes sprang an unexpected leak.

Jacko took up the chase. He beat Billy to the bottom of the stairs, and raced for the top. Four legs being better than two, he arrived first. He sat, tongue lolling, waiting for his slow coach companion to catch up.

As Billy's face levelled with Jacko's, the

dog tried to lick him, but Billy moved him gently aside. He went into his bedroom and threw himself on to his bed. Jacko slunk after him and waited until he'd settled, before climbing up beside him. A sandpaper tongue swished across Billy's cheek.

'You won't let me down.' Billy ruffled the dog's ears before Jacko slipped his head between his paws and let out a soft moan.

'Happy birthday, Billy!' his mum called from somewhere in the house. She peered around his bedroom door. 'Why the long face?' she asked, creasing her brow. 'You've been waiting for today for ages. What's happened?' She sat on his bed.

He rolled over and buried his face in the

pillow.

She stroked his hair. 'Billy,' she said lowering her voice, 'talk to me.'

'Grandad,' he whispered. He pressed his face into the pillow.

Jacko sneezed, as dogs often do for no apparent reason. Both Billy and his mum jumped. Billy stretched his arm out to smooth the dog's fur, but said nothing.

'What about Grandad? What's he done?' Mum asked.

'No money.'

'What do you mean no money?'

'It'll be some stupid present like usual. I asked him for money.'

'Billy, you can't make demands on him. People give presents because they want to, not because you asked. You don't know what he's got you. It'll be a surprise.' She sounded cheery as she tried to lift his spirits. 'You know you like surprises. What about—'

'Mum,' he said, cutting her off, 'it's because he's old. He has no idea what kids want.' He buried his face back in the pillow. The hollow feeling in his stomach remained.

'Be that as it may, you'd better buck up, young man! You've got guests arriving for your party in a few hours.' She tried to lift him into a sitting position but Billy clung to his pillow. Jacko jumped off the bed in anticipation.

'Okay, Jacko, I'm coming—' Billy's mum said as she stroked the dog's head. 'Now,

Billy, you've got to shower, dress and get yourself downstairs as quickly as you can. And no more Mr Grumpy!'

3

THE MAGIC OF A BIRTHDAY PARTY

'It's three o'clock.' No sooner had Billy spoken the words than the doorbell rang, followed by three hard raps of the knocker.

'Okay, keep your hair on.' Billy mumbled to himself, as he and Jacko reached the door together.

'Hi mate, I should have known it was you,' he said to Ant as he opened the door.

Ant gave Jacko a stroke as he passed. Max was close behind him. Seeing Jacko, she got down on her knees to give him a hug. He licked her face.

'Oi, I've had a wash today thanks!' Max said, wiping her cheek with her sleeve.

Soon the house pulsated with the sound of six boys, one girl, and a dog having fun. Blind-man's-buff proved popular, as did musical chairs. Sticking the tail on the donkey, with Jacko as the donkey, took on a new twist. Blindfolded, with one arm behind their backs, each child took turns to Sellotape a cardboard tail onto the boisterous dog that had little understanding of, or regard for, the game's rules.

'Okay, listen up.' Billy's mum clapped her hands to get their attention. 'If you go into the next room—' She raised her voice to compete against the noise. 'Boys, hush now. We have our entertainer, The Great Magisco!' She threw open her arms like theatre curtains unfolding. 'The Great Magisco will perform tricks the likes of which you've never seen before!' The drama in her voice got the children's attention.

The boys settled on the floor in the living room. The curtains were pulled shut. When Billy's mum turned off the small table lamp it went completely dark. The boys whistled and hooted.

The music began, low and haunting at first, then louder. As it reached a crescendo the lights came on and, as if by magic, The Great Magisco appeared.

It was Billy's grandad wearing a top hat

from the charity shop and a green plastic cape he used to keep the rain off while fishing. He was twirling a black walking stick for added effect.

He bowed deeply and with such force that his hat toppled forward. Quick as a flash, he caught it. He held out both hat and stick to his assistant, who was standing alongside him. Max, now in a pink tutu covered in sequins, sparkled as she moved.

The music faded. The Great Magisco spoke:

> *'I hope you're here in good cheer,*
> *To see and wonder at sights to behold,*
> *Magic is serious, magic is fun,*
> *But most of all,*
> *It has to be done with no disbelievers,*
> *I'm told ...'*

He raised his finger and pointed at Billy

and his friends. 'Do you all believe in magic?'

Each boy nodded; except Tom, who laughed.

'I see we have a doubter. Would you like me to turn you into a frog, boy?' The Great Magisco spoke in a deep rumble.

Tom stopped laughing while the others roared.

'Shush and we'll begin,'

The Great Magisco beckoned to his assistant Max. She passed him a pack of playing cards. He shuffled them twice, making large, elaborate gestures. The boys looked on, silent and unblinking.

Shaping the cards into a fan, The Great Magisco offered the pack to each boy in turn. 'Pick one card each,' he instructed.

'Now, don't show your card to me or anyone else. Take a look for yourself and then sit on it.' His voice was ferocious, almost a growl. Billy had never heard his grandad speak like this, nor had Jacko, who wandered up to Max looking for reassurance.

She tried to shove him away. 'I'm busy, silly.' She spoke in a whisper. 'It's okay; it's only Grandad, you old softy.'

The Great Magisco passed the remaining cards to his sequinned assistant. As he did, Jacko pushed his nose between Max's hands and the approaching pack of cards. The whole lot landed on the carpet, making the boys roar with laughter.

'You've spoiled it now,' Max told Jacko. He looked at her with his large, soulful brown eyes. 'Go on, shoo,' she said gently.

Billy half-rose from his seated position to call the dog. His mum was standing behind him for some reason. Jacko ignored them both. Standing, Billy patted his knees to get the dog to come. 'Sit, Jacko!' The dog groaned as he collapsed on the floor. Billy squatted beside him.

The Great Magisco made a knot in a piece of rope. Holding the rope by one end he shook it and the knot vanished. Everyone gasped and clapped. Then he made a coin disappear, only for it to reappear behind Ant's ear. There were more gasps and clapping.

'Now for my last trick,' said The Great Magisco.

As the lights dimmed, Max rolled a

newspaper into a long, thin tube. Billy's mum turned the lights up again while Max tipped the tube every which way so that all could see it was empty.

She passed it to The Great Magisco, who twirled it around, while swishing his cape for added drama.

'Abracadabra, see them fly. Watch the balls take to the sky!' Bringing the tube to his mouth, The Great Magisco made a mighty huff. Two ping-pong balls shot to the far side of the room.

One bounced off a picture frame, and Ant caught it. The other dropped down behind the sofa. Hot on its trail, Jacko squeezed into an impossible gap. True to his breed, he sniffed and snorted in the dust until he retrieved it.

As everyone clapped, The Great Magisco took Max's hand and they both bowed.

'That's all, except for singing "Happy Birthday" to Billy.' Grandad smiled at him. 'Maybe we should stand up to sing.'

All the boys stood.

With the lights on, Tom noticed something on the floor. 'Hey, what's that?' Tom pointed behind Billy. 'There behind you Billy, on the floor.'

'Yeah, yeah, good one. I'm not falling for that old trick.' Billy said, but he could not help taking a sneak peek.

He made a vacuum with his mouth, sucking all the air out of the room. 'Wow!' he exclaimed. His playing card was gone and a twenty-pound note, lay where he had been squatting.

'Grandad, look!' He waved the money over his head. 'Your magic worked! My card's gone, but see what I've got.' He ran to his grandad and clasped both arms around him. He held on with great force, making Grandad rock back and forth.

'Steady on or you'll push me over. I'm not as young as I used to be.' Grandad hugged him back. 'Isn't that what you wanted?'

'You're the best grandad ever. Thanks.'

'Now don't lose it. Put it up in your bedroom, safe away from Jacko.' Grandad fluffed Billy's hair.

On hearing his name, Jacko appeared with a mouthful of red and black striped sock, (the one Billy had lost months before), a pile of fluff and the missing ping-pong ball. Looking proud of himself, Jacko expected praise, but Billy was gone.

Billy had received his first ever twenty-pound note, for his tenth birthday, on the tenth day of the tenth month, from his only grandad! He ran up the stairs two at a time heading for his bedroom. He needed to make sure there was no mistaking the note for anyone else's money. He wrote his name on it in black ink: 'BILLY' followed by '10 10 10'.

4

BILLY AND ANT AT THE PARK

'Now, be careful Billy, keep off the main road, and remember to walk over the crossing. Traffic moves too fast near the park; you'd think they'd put speed bumps in ...' His mum's voice trailed away as the Billy and Ant sped off.

Once inside the park gates, the boys practised wheelies every time the coast was clear.

'This bike's awesome!' Billy was really happy with his main birthday present. He let out a 'Yahoo …!' as they sped across the park.

'Oi, Field. I hear you had a birthday party. Why didn't you invite me?' someone shouted.

Billy stopped dead in his tracks.

'Ant, come here, quick.' He covered his mouth with his hand so only Ant could hear. 'That's Tom's older brother Eddy, isn't it?'

Ant peered across at the three lads standing next to the swings. 'Looks like him, but I've no idea who he's with. I don't think we should go any nearer.' Ant said.

'Didn't you hear me?' Eddy growled, walking towards them, his mates tagging along behind. 'I *said* you had a birthday party and you didn't invite me. I think that's a bit rude.' His pace quickened.

'He only invited people from our class. Your brother Tom came,' Ant called back.

'I ain't talking to you, titch,' Eddy said, poking Ant in the chest. 'It's birthday boy here I've got a problem with.'

He glared at Billy, his jaw hardened. 'My brother says you got twenty quid from your magician grandad. Well I like magic only I ain't got a grandad cos he's dead. I think you should give me that twenty quid to show that you're sorry for my loss.'

He pressed his face up against Billy's. His breath smelled of mint gum and cigarettes. Billy pulled back. His new bike shifted off balance and he nearly dropped it.

'Oi, mind my trainers with that heap.' Eddy kicked the tyre. 'Now see what you've done! There's a big black mark right across the front of my trainers.' Eddy lifted his foot to show them.

Billy felt his stomach catapult and a lump formed in his throat. His heart beat faster with fear. He had never liked Eddy, and now he liked him even less.

'But *you* did that. You just kicked my tyre!' Billy said. He spoke without thinking.

'You calling me a liar?' Eddy's faced reddened, and he turned to his gang for support. 'Did you hear him?'

They all nodded in agreement.

'What you gonna do about it, Eddy?' the tallest one asked.

'I think I need to teach him a lesson in

manners, a hard lesson,' he snarled. 'It's not nice to go around calling people liars.' As he spoke, he poked Billy's arm. 'Didn't your mum teach you nothin? You've got a mum, haven't you? Oh that's right, she's that Deputy Head Teacher at our stupid school. A right old moaner she is, always barking at us.' Eddy pretended to be Billy's mum. 'Do this, don't do that.' He said in a comical high-pitched voice. 'Doesn't she drive you crazy at home?' Eddy laughed, as did his friends.

'I saw you kick the tyre,' Ant spoke, pulling himself up to his full height. 'Billy didn't do anything.'

Eddy spun around. 'When I want your opinion I'll ask for it.' He gave Ant a death glare. 'My gripe's with him,'—he jabbed

Billy's arm— 'not you, unless you want a slap as well.'

Ant held Eddy's stare for a moment before dropping his eyes. He stepped back a pace and focused on a spot on the ground. He felt really scared, and wanted to turn invisible.

'I'll tell you what, Billy Field, if you get on your bike NOW,' Eddy shouted the *now*, 'and ride back to your house to get that twenty quid for me, I'll forget all about this, and you won't get hurt.'

Eddy didn't wait for an answer. He looked at his watch. 'Be at the bottom of your road in fifteen minutes. Go on, get out of here! What are you waiting for? The clock's ticking—tic toc, tic toc.' Eddy swung at Billy, trying to slap him around the back of the head. He missed.

Billy and Ant rode away so fast their pedals were a blur. The sound of mocking laughter followed them.

'What are we gonna do, Billy?' Ant puffed. They kept up their fast pace.

'I've got no choice. When we get back to my place, don't say anything to my mum or dad, and especially not to Grandad if you see him.'

'But you can't say nothing! What if your mum asks what you've done with the money?'

They pulled up outside Billy's house. 'Just follow my lead,' Billy said.

'That was quick, boys. Nothing wrong, is there? You haven't got a puncture or anything like that?' Billy's mum looked at each of them in turn.

'No, nothing, Mum. I just forgot something, that's all. We'll be off again in a minute.' Billy passed straight through the kitchen, trailed by Ant. Jacko joined the procession.

The boys made their way to Billy's bedroom and he collected the twenty-pound note from his wooden pencil case where he had hidden it. Cramming it into his pocket, he and Ant marched straight back downstairs, through the kitchen, then out the back door.

Jacko followed behind, hoping they would take him with them.

'Sorry Jacko.' Billy stopped to give him a rub. Bending down, he whispered in his ear, 'I bet you could scare off those bullies.'

He stroked Jacko one more time. As he did, a tear trickled into the corner of his eye. The thought of giving up his twenty-pound note hit him hard.

'You all right, Billy? You look like you're crying,' his mum enquired.

Billy could not speak; his throat had closed over. He pulled the door shut.

'Billy!' she yelled, calling him back.

'No, course not.' He said as he approached her He squeezed the words out, 'One of Jacko's hairs jabbed me in the eye.' Billy rubbed at it, trying to hide his tears.

Billy saw the group of older boys waiting as he and Ant approached the end of the road.

'There they are.' Billy pointed towards the gang. Being smaller, Ant could not see over the cars until they were closer.

'Oh yeah, I see him now. What we gonna do?' Ant's eyes widened; he looked to Billy for guidance.

Different ideas galloped through Billy's mind before he settled on a plan.

'You stop before we reach them, and turn your bike around for a quick getaway. I'll pedal on, fling the twenty-pound note at Eddy, then keep going as fast as I can. If we split up they won't be able to chase us both.'

Billy looked at Ant to make sure he

understood. Ant returned his glance.

'Then, go straight home and we'll meet up as soon as we can,' Billy directed him.

Screwing up the courage, Billy drew alongside the boys. He hit his brakes hard, which screeched in response. A dust cloud hovered around his back tyre for a few moments before fading away. He halted for a split second, just long enough to throw the money at Eddy. Desperate to avoid capture, he pushed hard on his pedals. Watching for any flailing arms, hands or feet, he ducked past the other boys to make good his escape.

Billy pushed so hard his foot slipped off the pedal and the bike lurched to one side. He hit the ground with a thump; tears pricked his eyes. As he lay in a heap, he saw Eddy and his gang moving towards him. Ignoring the jabbing pain from his shin, Billy scrambled back onto his birthday bike.

'You haven't seen the last of me Billy boy.' The gruffness of Eddy's voice was unmistakable. 'Run, scaredy-cat, but don't forget I know where you live!' Eddy's words followed Billy as he made his getaway.

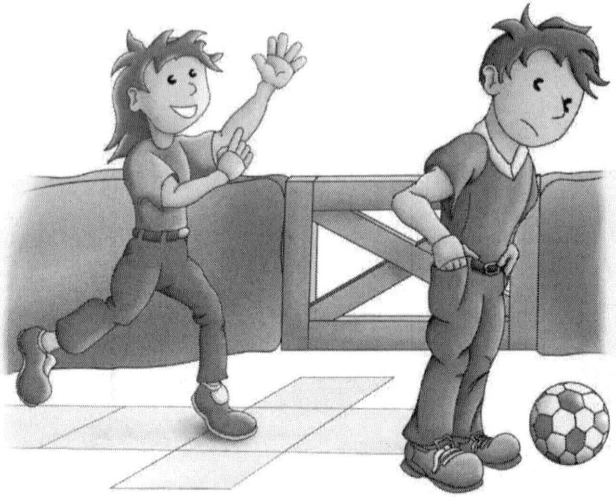

5

ANT TELLS MAX

Ant reached his house unscathed. Max was playing in the garden.

'Where's Billy?' she asked. 'I thought you two were going on a bike ride? I saw his new bike parked in the garage at the party. I want a yellow one. That's the colour of the sun, all bright and cheery. Colours should be cheerful, and yellow makes you happy.'

She stopped talking to catch her breath. 'Are you happy?' She looked into Ant's face as he walked past. 'You don't look happy. I'm happy. Why aren't all people happy? What's to be sad about?' She skipped down the path.

'Max, just shut up. His bike's blue. So what?'

She shrugged. 'I was only saying yellow's like the sun. Anyway, don't shout at me. It's not nice to shout. I've done nothing wrong.'

'Sorry sis, it's just that Billy and me had a bit of trouble at the park.'

'What? Who with?' She stopped smiling.

'Tom's brother Eddy.'

'What? Old stupid Eddy?'

'Shush! Don't let anyone hear you say that.' Ant looked around to make sure no one had heard. 'He stole Billy's twenty-pound note; the one his grandad magicked.'

'Why?'

'Cos Billy never invited him to his party. Eddy was really mad because he likes magic.'

'Well his sister Katie, she's in my class, and always calls him stupid. Apparently, he smokes around the back of the bike sheds, and everyone knows smoking's stupid. So he must be stupid too.' Max continued with her game of hopscotch.

'Are you good friends with Katie?'

'She's my …'—Max counted on her fingers—'… number six best friend. No wait, me and Sally fell out when she told

Miss I cheated in spelling. I didn't really cheat, it just happened I had 'danger' written on my hand from when I was learning words for the test. So Katie's my … one, two, three, four, five best friend.'

'Fifth, not five,' said Ant.

'That's what I said.' She held her hand up with all her fingers pointing upward. 'See, it's five.'

'Fine, five. Will you see Katie soon?'

'I've got swimming club tomorrow and she's usually there.' Max came to a halt. 'Why?'

'We need a plan to get Billy's money back before his grandad finds out it's been stolen.'

'Well,' Max said, continuing her

jumping, 'Katie told me that on Tuesday after school, her, Tom, and Eddy are all going to town to shop for school stuff. Their mum's taking them. Maybe you and Billy could learn to be pickpockets like in *Oliver Twist*. You could bump into Eddy when he's with his mum, and steal it back.' She beamed.

Ant looked at her. He was not sure her plan would work, but he did not have a better one. *We need help*, he thought to himself.

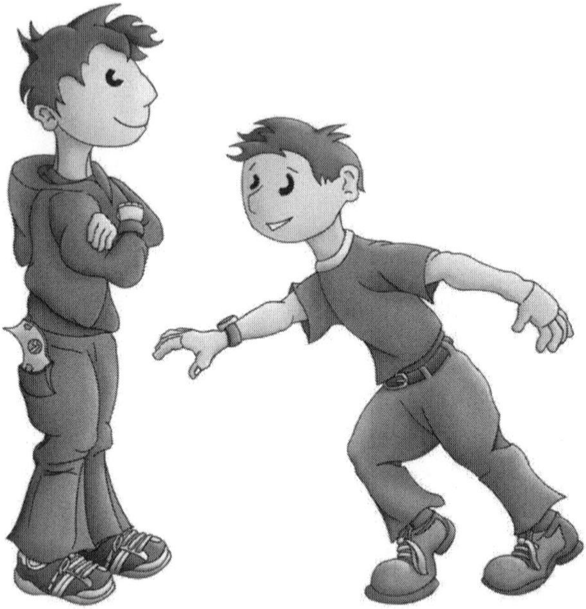

6

MAX HAS ANOTHER PLAN

Max had another idea and soon arrived at Billy's grandad's front door.

'Ah, my magic helper! I wondered who was knocking.' Billy's grandad tousled Max's hair.

'Please, Billy's grandad, I need to tell you something.' Max looked around to check that no one was listening.

'Well, don't just stand there, come on in. Only for a few minutes, mind, I'm off to

Billy's house for tea. We'll probably have leftovers from the party, curly sandwiches and stale cake. My daughter seems to think I'm a dustbin. It's true I hate waste. As my father would say, 'Waste not, want not.' We had none of this recycling stuff in my day. Nobody ever left anything! Most of the time there wasn't enough food to go around, never mind waste it.'

He sat in his large armchair while Max sat opposite him on the sofa. 'So what's so important, young lady?' Grandad asked.

Max built herself up, preparing to do what she knew she had to do. It was not going to be easy; the bubbling in her stomach told her so.

'Billy doesn't know I'm here, nor does

Ant.' She covered her mouth with her hand, fearful of being overheard. 'But I have a plan to get the money back.'

'Hold on, a plan? Money back? What are you talking about young lady?' Grandad creased his brow.

'You know Eddy, Tom's older brother, and Katie, his sister who's in my class, well he, that's Eddy, not Tom, of course—'

'No, of course.' Grandad bent forward, hoping it would improve his understanding.

'He stole the twenty pounds you magicked for Billy. And I have a plan to get it back.' She looked at him as if to say, *isn't it obvious?*

Leaning forward had not helped.

Grandad scratched his head.

'Am I hearing you right? Are you saying Billy had his present stolen by this Eddy boy?'

'Yes.' Max saw a flash of disappointment in Grandad's eyes.

He shook his head in disbelief. 'What's the world coming to?'

'Eddy's fourteen, nearly fifteen and he goes to Elliotts school, where Billy's mum is the head teacher.' Max offered.

'Deputy Head Teacher,' Grandad corrected her. 'Does Billy's mum know about Eddy? And does she know you're here?'

'My mum knows I'm here, but I told her it was about magic. She doesn't know about the lost money. No one does.'

'Lost or stolen? There's a big difference.' Grandad rubbed his chin. 'Did Billy lose it and Eddy find it?'

'Not according to Ant,' said Max, 'He said Eddy stole it when they were at the park.' She looked to see if he'd understood. 'So I suggested they pickpocket Eddy on Tuesday after school when he's in town with Katie and Tom buying their school uniforms. Well, I'm not sure what they're buying actually, but his mum will be there. Then I thought of your magic, so that's why I'm here.' Max flopped back on the sofa, relieved to have completed her story.

'Hmm, magic you say ...' Grandad wiped his hand around the back of his neck. 'What exactly is your plan?'

Max's excitement showed in the twinkling of her eyes. 'Well, Ant said Eddy took the money since he wasn't invited to the party, and 'cos he missed your magic show.' Max stopped talking to rummage around in her pocket before pulling out a folded sheet of paper. 'Here.' She smoothed the sketch and held it up. 'It's not finished yet, but it won't take long. I need to do a bit more colouring.' She waved it about.

'Hold still, what is it?' Grandad was more confused than ever. He knew he had to hear her story to the finish, seeing how eager she was to tell him her secret plan to magic the twenty-pound note.

Max held out the drawing. 'I've only

done it from memory, but it's a twenty-pound note. Look, there's the two and there's the nothing.' Her finger darted between the two figures.

'It's a zero, not nothing.' Grandad said helpfully.

Now Max looked confused.

'Oh, it doesn't matter. So you're suggesting we take your twenty-pound note and swap it for the real thing?'

'Using your magic! Like you made the playing card turn into money. That way Billy gets his money back and Eddy—'

'—ends up with a drawing. You're not expecting him to think it's an actual twenty-pound note, are you?'

'No, course not. It's to teach him a

lesson.' Max said.

'And this will happen Tuesday, you say?'

'Yeah. I'm seeing Katie tomorrow.'

'Not Tuesday?' Grandad returned to feeling confused.

'At swimming. It's always swimming club on Monday.' Max wondered why he couldn't follow her.

Grandad felt his understanding of the situation fading away.

'Billy's grandad, you need to concentrate.' She waited for the lines on his forehead to smooth before continuing. 'At swimming I'll ask Katie if I can go shopping with her and her mum on Tuesday. You come to town, too. The uniform shop is in the shopping centre.' Max spoke slowly, 'I'll meet you under the clock; you know the big one where all those soldiers march around swinging their arms.' Her face lit up at the thought. 'Then I'll come and find you.'

'Yes, I know the clock, I've taken Billy there many times. Then what?' He looked at her expectantly.

'We'll find Eddy and then you make the money jump out of his pocket or something.' She shrugged her shoulders. 'I don't know. You're the one who does magic!'

'I think I need to give your plan more thought, but I'll certainly meet you under the clock. I'm afraid now I have to get ready to go to tea.' Grandad stood. He held out his hand to help Max to her feet.

Max slipped down from the sofa. 'Don't say anything to Billy. Promise!' She looked directly at Billy's Grandad. 'Ant says Billy's really upset and it wasn't his fault. It was stupid Eddy's.'

I wonder how stupid Eddy really is, Grandad thought. He opened the door for Max. 'Bye, dear, we'll sort this out.' He waved to her. 'Straight home now. See you Tuesday in the shopping centre at four o'clock.'

When Billy woke on Monday morning, his mum was in her study surrounded by piles of paper, and did not want to be disturbed.

He sat at the kitchen table and played with his cereal, stirring it around the bowl. His eyes felt puffy from a night of crying. He moved all the cereal to one side and took a spoonful of sugary milk. He pushed at the cereal again with his spoon. Jacko sat watching him.

'It's not fair,' he said as Jacko licked his hand. 'You watch. When I'm older I'll get my own back.' The full-length body strokes Billy was giving Jacko were more out of frustration than love. 'What can I do?'

Jacko yawned.

'Sorry Jacks, am I boring you?' Sarcasm was lost on the dog. 'You sure you've got no ideas? And don't say tell Mum or Dad. I can't 'cos if I do, Grandad'll find out.' He fought hard to hold back fresh tears. 'I hate Eddy.'

Ant's face appeared at the kitchen window, his jacket collar pulled up against the morning chill. He tapped on the glass. 'Come on, it's blinking freezing out here.' Ant mouthed through the window.

'It's unlocked.' Billy's voice sounded like a feeble old man's.

Ant let himself in and started speaking straightaway. 'I've been thinking about what Max said. You know, about becoming pickpockets. I tried it on her and got a sweet. She never felt a thing.' Ant stood as tall as he could. 'It's all about distraction.'

A smile filled Ant's face. 'Go on, stand up.' He pushed on Billy's shoulder. 'I'll

BILLY HAS A BIRTHDAY

show you. Come on.' Ant had created his own drawing of a twenty-pound note. He passed it to Billy. 'Put that in your pocket.'

Billy stood by the kitchen table and Ant walked towards him acting all cool. He banged into his friend's shoulder. 'Oh, sorry mate.'

Using the distraction, Ant fumbled around, trying to get his fingers into Billy's trouser pocket. Jacko had other ideas and pushed between them, defending his master. Both boys started to laugh.

Billy stopped giggling and dropped his head. 'What the flip was that about? If you do that to Eddy Jost you won't be laughing for long. Any other ideas?'

'Not really, but Max said Tom, Katie and

Eddy will be in town tomorrow after school with their mum. Max is going to see the clock with Katie. You know, the one with the soldiers.' Ant waited for a response.

'So?' Billy could hardly bring himself to speak.

'If we go, we can tell Eddy's mum what he did and she'll get it back for us.'

Billy curled his top lip.

Ant was desperate to help his best friend. 'I know it's not great, and maybe she won't believe us, but I'm not sure we've got any other choice.' He put a hand on Billy's shoulder. 'Sorry mate.'

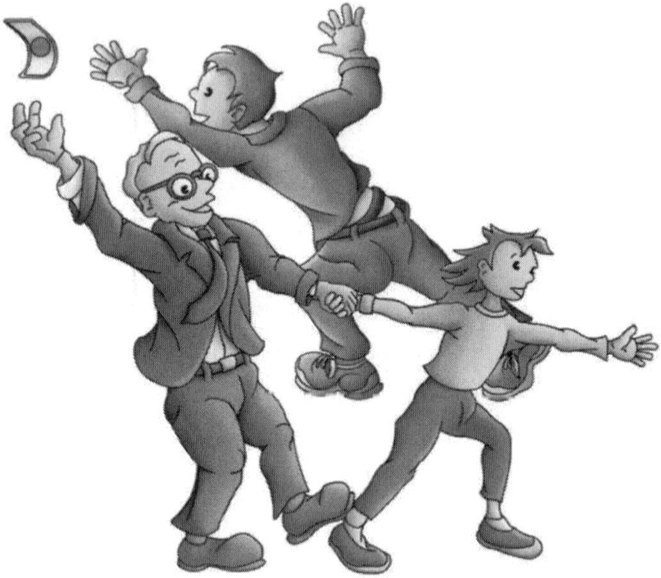

7

THE GREAT MAGISCO

'Come on, Mum, I'm not a kid. I've seen that clock loads of times. Those stupid soldiers marching about ... do I have to?' Eddy protested as he pushed open the large glass doors to the shopping centre.

'You're not the only person in this family. Katie and Tom want to see it, and Max too I imagine. If we don't hurry we'll miss it striking the hour.'

Eddy pushed Tom. 'Baby brother wants to see the soldiers,' he mocked.

'Hey, enough of that. You were always begging me to take you to see it.' Eddy's mum glared at him.

'Yeah, when I was five maybe; I'll be fifteen next month.'

'Well, you're still my baby.' She grabbed his cheek. 'Coochie coo.'

'Oi, get off.' He jerked his head away.

'We're going to get something to eat after seeing the clock. I'm guessing you're not too grown up to eat with us?' His mum said, thinking food would win him over.

'No thanks, I'm meeting my friends. We're off for a burger.' Eddy hooked his fingers into the waistband of his jeans, pulling them up just enough to cover his boxer shorts.

'Oh, okay. So where are you getting the money from?' his mum asked.

Shuffling his feet, Eddy dropped his gaze and focused on the floor. The clock came into view, and he could see several people gathered underneath it. Eddy saw his gang standing off to one side looking like they were not interested.

'Well?' his mum asked again.

Eddy mumbled back as though he had a mouthful of mashed potato, saying something about a paper round before mooching off.

🐾 🐾

Max spotted Billy's grandad. 'Billy's grandad!' she called, her eyes widened. 'I'm here!' She ran ahead of the group and reached him just as the clock struck four.

At each strike, from a door in the clock face, carved wooden figures dressed in red tunics, black trousers and boots moved forward to present arms. The intricate mechanism whirred and chattered as soldier followed soldier, moving around an elaborate track before disappearing for another hour.

Katie's mum, Katie, and Tom came to stand by Max. 'This is Billy's grandad,' Max said. 'He does magic.'

'I know Tom here.' Grandad shook Tom's hand. 'This young man said he didn't believe in magic. But I think he changed his mind.' He smiled at Tom.

Tom returned his smile.

'Max said she was meeting you here.' Katie's mum looked to Grandad for confirmation.

'She's my assistant.' Grandad put his arm round Max's shoulder. 'We've an important magic trick to perform.' She beamed up at him.

'We're going to get something to drink first,' Max said. She had her eye on Eddy, who was standing several feet away talking to his gang. 'Quick, we need to go—this way.' She pulled on Grandad's jacket. 'Bye Katie!'

Grandad said goodbye to the others as he got dragged away.

No one saw Ant and Billy arrive with Jacko on a lead.

Max signalled to Billy's Grandad to bend down. She put her mouth close to his ear. 'I heard them say they're going to get a burger. We need to catch them up.' Still holding Grandad's jacket, she led the way.

Eddy and his mates were close to the front door of the burger bar by the time Max and Grandad got close.

'Which one's Eddy?' Grandad peered at the group of teenage boys.

'Him! The one with his jeans hanging down.' Max pointed in the direction of Eddy.

'He needs a belt by the look of it.'

'Don't be silly, Billy's Grandad, that's the fashion.'

'Well not for me it's not. Trousers should be worn at the waist,' said Grandad.

'Come on quick, they're going in.' Max went first. They joined the queue behind the lads, standing close enough to eavesdrop.

The lads were too busy messing about to notice Max and Billy's Grandad.

'It's your treat, Eddy, since you nicked the money,' one of his gang said.

'I didn't exactly nick it, he sort of gave it to me,' Eddy replied. All the boys laughed.

'Yeah, otherwise you'd have given him a beating.' More laughter followed.

'So where's this famous twenty-pound note?' another of the lads asked.

Max stood on her tiptoes, 'Hope he shows it,' she whispered, trying to see.

Grandad shushed her. 'He'll hear you.'

Eddy slapped his thigh where his jeans pocket was located.

Without warning, Max reached up and tapped Eddy's arm. He whirled around, looking first at Billy's grandad and then at her.

'What?' Eddy grunted.

'You said you like magic,' Max said.

'Who wants to know?' Eddy's eyes darted between the pair.

Grandad took over the conversation. 'I've heard you were upset about not being invited to Billy Field's birthday party.'

'What are you going on about?' Eddy looked them up and down before turning back to his mates.

Grandad tapped his shoulder. 'What my assistant and I are trying to say is we understand you like magic, so we're here to do a trick for you.' Grandad remained calm even though Eddy appeared menacing.

Eddy looked back at him. 'Are you serious?' He turned towards to his gang. 'This bloke's off his rocker.' They all sniggered.

The queue moved forward. Soon they would have to order and pay for their meals. Max tugged at Grandad's jacket. 'Go on do it now or it'll be too late.'

'So, Eddy,' Grandad started.

Eddy turned once more to face them.

'You've a twenty-pound note, I understand.'

'Who told you? Mind your own business.' Eddy jerked his head around to see who might be listening. Max saw his leg begin to shake.

'Would you like another one … for free?' Grandad offered.

'What, you'd give me twenty quid for nothing? You're joking me.' An easy grin spread over Eddy's face.

'No, not at all, it's magic.' Grandad sounded very matter of fact.

'If I say yes will you go away?' Eddy laughed at his own words along with his mates.

'Sure, the trick won't take long. All I need is your twenty-pound note.' Grandad looked into Eddy's eyes. 'You do trust me, don't you?'

'What, an old bloke like you?' Eddy stared back, unsure what was going to happen. 'Here.' He dug into his pocket to retrieve the crumpled note. 'Let's see what you can do with that. I want it back, mind you.'

Max slipped her hand-drawn note to Billy's grandad, and he slid it up his sleeve. Taking the real note from Eddy, Grandad held it up for all to see.

'My, the Queen wouldn't be happy to see what you've done to her money.' Using slow, deliberate movements, Grandad proceeded to smooth it out, before he held it over his head.

The queue was restless. Shouts of 'Come on, move up,' and 'I'm hungry' followed.

Unmoved, Grandad as The Great Magisco, pivoted left and right, showing off the note to anyone who cared to look. As part of the act, he made the growling noise that came from deep in his chest.

He whispered to Max, 'When I say *now*, grab my hand and we'll make a dash for it.' She smiled and nodded.

'Abracadabra,' he said, waving his hands and making exaggerated movements. 'On the head of my mother, let this note turn into another!' Grandad pushed his hands upward and outward.

He let Max's drawing fly. It rose into the air above Eddy's head. All eyes turned to watch it.

'Now!' Grandad grabbed Max's outstretched hand and fled. He held her tight as they ran for the exit.

Once outside, they sprinted towards the clock.

'I'm a fast runner,' said Max. She could hear Billy's grandad panting. 'Are you okay?'

'We're … nearly … there.' Grandad breathed heavily. 'There's the clock.' He looked about. 'Can you see Katie's mum anywhere?' He stopped to scan the nearby shops and restaurants, but she was nowhere in sight.

'Come on, Billy's grandad, look who's over there.' Max pointed to two police officers gazing into a shop window. 'It's PC Wright! He's often on our street.' She clapped her hands in glee. 'He always talks to me.' She ran towards the policemen.

Grandad slowed to a stop. Propped up against a wall, he held his chest. He was struggling for breath; beads of perspiration formed on his brow, and he was starting to feel unwell.

🐕 🐕

'Look, there he is! Hey, old man!' Eddy's shout alerted Grandad to his approach, Eddy's jeans slipping down delayed his arrival.

'So what's this, then?' Eddy shoved

Max's drawing in Grandad's face. 'You thought you could swindle me?' He bounced on his toes like a boxer warming up. 'Me, Eddy Jost? Don't you know who I am?' He jabbed his fist into the air, missing Grandad's face by a few inches. 'No one messes with me! No one! Do you hear me?'

Eddy poked Grandad's chest. 'Give me my money and we'll call it quits. Otherwise …!' Spittle flowed from his lips as he spoke and his eyebrows knotted together. To make sure Grandad got the message he followed up with a series of air jabs.

Eyes facing straight ahead, Grandad never blinked. He watched Eddy's antics with a mixture of sorrow and amusement. Sorrow as he knew Eddy was young and that such behaviour would get him into trouble in the years to come; and amusement because with each bounce Eddy's trousers slipped further down.

Out of the corner of his eye, Grandad saw Max leading two burly police officers over.

Grandad's silence and lack of retaliation frustrated Eddy even more.

'Don't mess with me.' Eddy said, their faces almost touching. 'Give me my money now!' The veins on his forehead stood out. Losing control, he pulled his arm back. He held his clenched fist at shoulder height.

Before Eddy could release a punch, PC Wright, with the skill of a champion wrestler, slipped his hand into the crook shape made by Eddy's arm. Following through, he had Eddy's head pinned up against the wall, his arms pulled back behind him, and his legs stretched wide.

'Get off me!' Unaware he was dealing with a police officer, Eddy wriggled to break loose. The ratcheting sound of closing handcuffs put paid to that. His struggle was over.

'I have to caution you,' said PC Wright, 'you do not have to say anything, but it may harm your defence if you do not mention when questioned something which you later rely on in court. Anything you do say may be given in evidence. Do you understand?' The police officer waited for Eddy to speak. 'And while you're at it, get your mum to buy you a belt to keep your trousers up or I'll add indecent exposure to the charges.'

The sound of sirens penetrated the shopping centre. Billy and Ant heard them, as did everyone else in the area.

'Let's take a look,' Ant said, leading the way. He set off in the direction of the commotion. He jumped onto a bench seat to get a better view. 'Hey look, it's your grandad!'

Billy took off at top speed. Jacko pulled hard on his lead until Billy lost his grip. Jacko vanished into the crowd.

'Grandad!' Billy was stuck behind a line of people all jostling to get a better view. 'I'm here!' Billy's heart thumped in his chest. He pushed with all his might to force his way to the front, but he was stopped by a police officer. 'It's my grandad! Please let me see him.' Billy blinked back the fear.

'Is this your sister?' The policeman was holding Max's hand.

'Yes, I mean no. Not really.' Confused, Billy just wanted to reach his grandad. 'She's my mate's sister.' Billy glanced at Max. 'What are you doing here?'

'We got your twenty pounds back from Eddy.' She could not get the words out fast enough. 'And PC Wright arrested him.' She pointed towards a handcuffed Eddy. He could see Tom, Katie, and their mum standing beyond him.

A paramedic tried to examine Grandad but Jacko grabbed the red blanket she had wrapped him in.

'It's okay, boy. She's a friend,' Billy said reassuringly.

The dog did not look convinced and bared his teeth at the paramedic just in case.

Grandad looked overwhelmed. Everything had moved so fast, but at least he had managed to get Billy's money back.

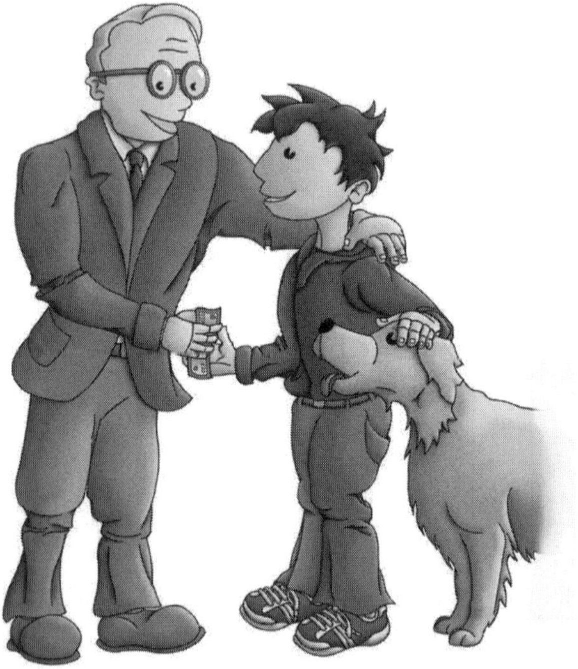

8

THE WRONG TWENTY-POUND NOTE

'Billy, why didn't you tell us?' his mum asked when they were all safely home. 'I know Eddy Jost only too well. He's always in trouble at school; he's been excluded several times.'

Billy looked down at his hands feeling happy the whole thing was over but guilty he had not told his parents he was in trouble. At least Grandad knew he had not lied about losing the money.

'As for The Great Magisco,' Billy's mum

turned to Grandad. 'What if he'd punched you or something? You're too old for stunts like that. But thanks all the same Dad.' She gave her father a hug.

Billy's mum then looked to Max; she was sat at the table tucking into a bowl of her favourite ice cream. 'We have Max here to thank; she saved the day.'

Max smiled up at them between spoonfuls.

'Oh Billy, before I forget,'—Grandad opened his wallet and removed a brand-new crisp twenty-pound note, taken from a cashpoint—'here's your twenty pounds. Now take it straight up to your bedroom and put it safely away.'

'Thanks, Grandad.' He wrapped his arms around him. 'And thanks, Max! I'll do it right now.' He ran out of the room, heading for the stairs. Before he reached them, he let out a cry of pain. 'Grandad!' His stomach clenched like a vice. He ran back to where they were.

'It's not mine!' He held out the note. The others moved in to get a closer look.

'What do you mean it's not yours?' his mum asked.

'See, here,' he said, pointing at the note, 'my name's missing. I wrote 'BILLY 10 10 10' in black ink on the Queen's neck, just under her chin.'

His elation evaporated, and a sense of despair returned. No longer standing upright, he rounded his shoulders and slouched off towards his bedroom. He wanted to be alone.

'Billy, come here, please.' Grandad's voice was calm. 'I need to tell you something.'

'What?' Billy didn't even bother to turn around.

'Listen to your Grandad, Billy,' his mum said. 'I'm sure there's a good explanation.'

Billy stood in front of Grandad, his eyes cast to the ground. He did not want to hear any explanation; he just wanted *his* twenty-pound note back.

'Eddy Jost is a bad lad.' Grandad shifted his gaze to Billy's mum, who nodded in agreement. 'He's in real trouble for what he's done and the police want to take him to juvenile court. To do that they need to ask you and Ant some questions about what happened in the park. Is that clear?'

Grandad waited for a response.

Billy muttered something and nothing, it was little more than a few grunts.

'Speak up, Billy. Grandad can't hear so well.' His Mum reminded him.

'Yes. Can I go now?' Billy turned to leave. Grandad caught hold of his arm.

'Not yet, I haven't finished. As well as asking you questions, I need to make a statement—that's what the police call it—about what happened. And since the whole thing revolves around your twenty-pound note, they've kept it.'

'What, *my* twenty-pound note? Why?' Billy stared at him, his eyes wide.

'Because it's important; it's evidence,' Grandad continued.

'Will they take fingerprints and put it

under one of the machines with a blue light to see if they match Eddy's?' The idea raced away with Billy. 'Will they have to take my fingerprints? And Ant's?' He inspected his hands, trying to remember which one he used to hold the note. 'What about my writing?' He looked at his mum and then back to Grandad. 'You know, because I wrote on it. Will I be in trouble with the Queen?'

'Hey, slow down, Sherlock Holmes.' Grandad was glad to hear him asking questions.

'Yeah, but what about Jacko here? He could have touched it!' Jacko sat by Billy. 'Will they want his paw prints?' They both looked down at the dog. He raised a paw.

'See, he knows.' Billy took Jacko's paw.

'You're a rascal,' Grandad said, glancing at Billy's mum. 'I see my favourite grandson is back.'

'Does that mean my note's gone forever?' Billy sighed heavily.

'Only until Eddy's been to court, but it might be awhile. So in the meantime I've given you a new one.' Grandad smiled at Billy. 'You know it doesn't matter about it not being the actual note. What's important is that you've got the money to spend as you want. Eddy will have to pay for what he's done. Bullying, stealing, and threatening behaviour can't be allowed. Let's hope he's learned a lesson.'

Grandad took hold of Billy's shoulders. 'Come on, Billy lad, smile. It's not as bad as all that.' He tickled Billy's ribs.

Squirming, Billy couldn't stop a laugh escaping. He wriggled to get away. Jacko joined in the fun, barking enthusiastically.

Billy really wanted *his* twenty-pound note to remind him of his once-in-a-lifetime tenth birthday on the tenth day of the tenth month. He felt pleased he could count on his family and friends in times of trouble. And he still had Grandad's twenty pounds to spend on a special birthday present.

THE END

GET YOUR FREE ACTIVITY BOOK

To accompany all the Billy Books there is a free activity book for each title. Each book includes word search, crossword, secret message and cryptogram puzzles plus pictures to colour.

To claim your **free** activity book go to the website **www.thebillybooks.co.uk** and click the button **Claim Your Free Activity Book**. Enter the code **BILLY7058** plus your name and email address.

BOOK REVIEW

If you found this book helpful, leaving a review on Goodreads.com or other book related websites would be appreciated by me and others who have yet to read it.

WHAT CHILDREN CAN LEARN FROM 'BILLY HAS A BIRTHDAY'

Bullying is a big problem for children today. Bullies look confident and strong; that is why they are intimidating. They cannot let their guard down because that would make them seem weak, and would reduce their power and sense of control. So they keep behaving as if they are very important people, while inside they are just like everyone else. They are, in fact, acting the part of someone who is confident and strong; acting as if they have power over others. And of course, they surround themselves with people who are like them—just in case they need reinforcements! That's the power of bullies—they are not often on their own. Simply standing your ground and confronting them often make things even worse because they have to defend their position to save face and the only way they know how to do that is by doing more of what they are already doing. Speaking out and reaching out to someone you trust is one way for you to deal with bullies. You might not be able to rid the world of bullies, but you can do something about how you deal with them.

In this story, Billy, like any other child, is looking forward to a big birthday. However, the local bullies hear he's been given a twenty-pound note and challenge him to hand it over. Billy realises he cannot fight the gang so has to agree to their demands. At first, Billy does not dare tell a grown-up, as he feels guilty about losing his birthday money. So, he and his friend Ant try to hatch a plan on their own to get it back. But it's not until Max, Ant's sister, hears about the problem that she realises an adult needs to be involved. She feels that Grandad who did the party magic and gave Billy the money in the first place, is the ideal person to confide in. Confident he'll know what to do, Max thinks up a plan and Grandad helps her. The bullies don't realise what is happening until it's too late. Grandad recovers the twenty-pound note, leaving the bullies to be dealt with by the authorities.

As Billy learned, the best way to deal with bullies is to reach out and ask for help from people you trust, and who have more experience —in this case his Grandad. He learns that to overcome bullying you have to have a strategy and get help. Putting up a fight just brings more difficulties, and might even put you in danger.

Notice also in the story that Billy felt guilty about having lost the twenty-pound note to the bullies, which made him nervous about confessing what had happened. When his mum asked him if he was okay, he had to lie to her, as he was frightened to tell her the truth. Making you feel nervous, anxious, or scared gives the bullies more ammunition to try to control you. If Billy could have confided in his mum or grandad straight away, he would have been able to get the help he needed and perhaps resolve the problem much sooner.

It takes courage to deal with difficult situations. Courage comes from within you; it is knowing that you deserve to be respected and treated fairly.

If you're horrible to me I'm going to write a song about it and you won't like it. That's how I operate. —**Taylor Swift**

Courage is fire, and bullying is smoke. —**Benjamin Disraeli**

BOOK 2

BILLY AND ANT FALL OUT

James Minter

Helen Rushworth – Illustrator

www.thebillybooks.co.uk

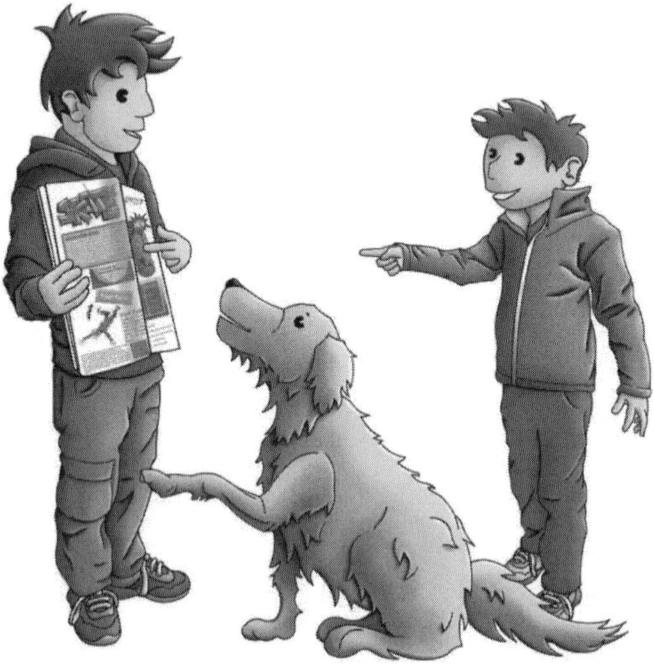

1

BILLY AND ANT FALL OUT

'Have you seen this?' Billy pointed at the skateboard magazine, while his dog Jacko, licked his paw. 'It's awesome. It's got go-faster wheels with extra special bearings. It'll go really fast.'

Billy rubbed Jacko's head, 'Shall I get you one? I've seen loads of dogs on YouTube riding skateboards. I'm sure you can do it; you're a clever boy.' He hugged

Jacko around the neck. 'Yes you are.' He buried his face in the dog's soft golden fur.

Billy stood up. 'Come on, boy. Up.' He patted himself on the chest. 'Come on, right up.'

Jacko stood on his hind legs and rested his front paws on Billy's shoulders. 'See, I said you were clever.'

The back door latch clicked, and both Billy and Jacko turned to see who was there. Ant, Billy's best friend, walked in.

'What are you two doing? Ant said, 'Practicing ballroom dancing? D'you know why dogs don't make good dancers? Because they've got two left feet!' Ant laughed.

Billy made a cheesy grin face. Jacko stayed where he was.

'Anyway, who's the girl out of you two?' Ant continued.

'You're the only girl around here,' Billy said, swinging a playful punch at Ant's arm.

Jacko dropped to the ground and woofed. Ant hit Billy back, and Jacko woofed again.

'Shush, Jacks, we're only messing.' Billy knelt beside him. 'Me and Ant are best mates.' He looked towards Ant, who was staring at the magazine. 'Aren't we?'

'What? Sorry mate, have you seen this skateboard? It's well nice. I'd love one like that.' Ant picked up the magazine and hugged it. He was off in a dream world where he was skateboarding like a professional.

'Yeah, but look at the price!' Billy said bringing his friend back to reality. 'It'll take two birthdays and a Christmas to save for it.'

They both looked longingly at the picture. Billy dreamed of the day he might own one.

'We'll get one, you'll see.' Ant sounded sure, but he had no idea if or when it might happen.

Billy turned to Ant. 'I know, let's promise that whoever gets a board first lets the other have a go.'

They held out their crooked little fingers and hooked them together. 'I promise,' they said together.

Billy looked down at Jacko as the dog pushed his way in between them. 'But I don't think you'll be riding a board for a while, and at that price, neither will I.'

Jacko only panted as Billy closed the magazine.

'So, what are we doing today?' Billy looked to Ant for inspiration.

'Fancy a bike ride?' Ant offered.

'Yeah, maybe, but not down the park.' Billy cringed at the thought of running into the bully who had stolen his birthday money a few weeks ago.

'Why not? Eddy won't be there.'

'No, but his gang will be. I don't want to risk it right now—let's give it a while longer.' Billy felt his stomach churn. 'Mum reckons Eddy'll get sent to a youth detention centre for bullying us and stealing my birthday money.'

'So where to then?' Ant shoved his hands deep into his jacket pockets. 'Before we go anywhere, I need to go home for some gloves.' Ant made a loud 'Brrr,' and shivered all over.

'What do you need gloves for? It's like midsummer out there, you big baby!' Billy scoffed.

'It's November, actually, and my mum says I've got bad circulation in my hands and feet. They get really cold.' Ant held up his hands. 'See, they're all blotchy red and blue already.'

'Oh, diddums, you got freezing *fingees* and *tootsies*?' Billy sneered. 'Let me have a look.' He walked towards his friend.

'No, you're not being nice. It's not my fault, and anyway, they *hurt* when they get cold.' Taking a step back, Ant folded his arms, burying his hands beneath his armpits.

'You're such a baby.' Billy mocked. 'How are you going to cycle like that? You won't even be able to reach the handlebars. I'll have to go without you if your *fingees* are too cold,'

'Why are you being so nasty?' Ant sounded confused. He looked at his hand again just to make sure.

'I'm not; you just need to grow up. All that *my mum says* stuff is really babyish.'

'Yeah, well, you can go for a bike ride by yourself, Billy Field.' Ant's anger crackled in his chest. 'You can be pretty mean.' Ant turned and headed towards the back door, but Jacko got there before him. 'Sorry, Jacks, I've got to go.' He gently moved the dog aside. 'Not sure when I'll see you again.' Ant stroked the dog one more time. The click of the latch confirmed that he had left.

'Good riddance to bad rubbish!' Billy shouted after him. He knelt beside Jacko.

'Who needs him, anyway? Come on boy, let's go walkies.'

'I wasn't expecting to see you back so soon.' Ant's mum was hanging out the washing as Ant rode into the garden. 'Where's Billy? I thought you two would be out on your bikes.'

Ant rode past his mum, stopping at the garden shed. He said nothing.

'Ant … Anthony, come here now!'

Ant meandered across the garden; his hands plunged into his pockets. 'What?'

'Don't *what* me. I was talking to you. What do you have to say for yourself?' His mum's face had lost its usual smile.

'Nothing.' He dropped his head and started to kick a stone between his feet.

'I asked you a question, and I expect an answer.' She brought her eyes level with his.

'Hi, Mum. Hi, Ant.' Maxine, Ant's younger sister said as she skipped up the garden. 'What are you doing, Ant? I thought you were going to Billy's.' She skipped on by.

'Not now, Max dear,' called her mum, but Max was already out of earshot. Ant started to wander off, too.

'Not so fast, young man. You've not answered my question.' His mum folded her arms across her chest.

'It's nothing Mum, really.'

'Well, if it's nothing you won't mind telling me.' She stood her ground.

'Billy,' Ant mumbled into his socks.

'What about Billy?'

'He called me a baby and said I needed to grow up.' Ant shifted his weight from foot to foot.

'That's not like him. You two are best friends.'

'We were.' Ant's eyes sprang an unexpected leak.

'What have you done to upset him?' His mum looked stern.

'Why is it always my fault? Even when Max does something wrong, I get the blame. It's not fair.' Ant let out a loud sigh.

'Look, no one's blaming you for anything. I'm just trying to find out what happened between you and Billy.'

'It's because I said I needed gloves.'

'Gloves!' She looked quizzical. 'What's wrong with needing gloves?'

'My hands get cold.'

'Of course they do, you've got poor circulation.'

'That's what I told him.' Ant shoved his hands deeper into his pockets.

'And that's why you two fell out?' His mum shook her head.

'He's ten now and he thinks I should be more grown up, like him. I can't help when my birthday is.' Tears rolled down Ant's cheek.

'Here.' She put her arms around him. 'You're my big boy, now, no more of this. Anyway, you've got Max to play with.'

'Yeah, but she's a girl.' As he spoke, he spun on one foot and wandered off towards the front gate dragging his toes along the stone garden path. He walked past Max, who had just finished visiting their rabbit, Cinders.

'What's wrong with him, Mum?' Max smiled up at her.

'Oh, he just wants to be grown up,' she replied.

I HOPE YOU ENJOYED THIS FREE CHAPTER. READ BOOK 2 TO FIND OUT WHAT HAPPENED BETWEEN BILLY AND ANT...

FOR PARENTS, TEACHERS, AND GUARDIANS: ABOUT THE 'BILLY BOOKS' SERIES

Billy and his friends are children entering young adulthood, trying to make sense of the world around them. Like all children, they are confronted by a complex, diverse, fast-changing, exciting world full of opportunities, contradictions, and dangers through which they must navigate on their way to becoming responsible adults.

What underlies their journey are the values they gain through their experiences. In early childhood, children acquire their values by watching the behaviour of their parents. From around eight years old onwards, children are driven by exploration, and seeking independence; they are more outward looking. It is at this age they begin to think for themselves, and are capable of putting their own meaning to feelings, and the events and experiences they live through. They are developing their own identity.

The Billy Books series supports an initiative championing Values-based Education, (VbE) founded by Dr Neil Hawkes*. The VbE objective is to influence a child's capacity to succeed in life by encouraging them to adopt positive values that will serve them during their early lives, and sustain them throughout their adulthood. Building on the VbE objective, each Billy book uses the power of traditional storytelling to contrast negative behaviours with positive outcomes to illustrate, guide, and shape a child's understanding of the importance of values.

This series of books help parents, guardians and teachers to deal with the issues that challenge children who are coming of age. Dealt with in a gentle way through storytelling, children begin to understand the challenges they face, and the importance of introducing positive values into their everyday lives. Setting the issues in a meaningful context helps a child to see things from a different perspective. These books act as icebreakers, allowing easier communication between parents, or other significant adults, and children when it comes to discussing difficult subjects. They are suitable for KS2, PSHE classes.

There are eight books are in the series. Suggestions for other topics to be dealt with in this way are always welcome. To this end, contact the author by email: james@jamesminter.com.

*Values-Based Education, (VbE) is a programme that is being adopted in schools to inspire adults and pupils to embrace and live positive human values. In English schools, there is now a Government requirement to teach British values. More information can be found at: www.valuesbasededucation.com/

BOOK 1 - BILLY HAS A BIRTHDAY

Bullies appear confident and strong. That is why they are scary and intimidating. Billy loses his birthday present, a twenty-pound note, to the school bully. With the help of a grown-up, he manages to get it back and the bully gets what he deserves.

BOOK 2 - BILLY AND ANT FALL OUT

False pride can make you feel so important that you would rather do something wrong than admit you have made a mistake. In this story, Billy says something nasty to Ant and they row. Ant goes away and makes a new friend, leaving Billy feeling angry and abandoned. His pride will not let him apologise to his best friend until things get out of hand.

BOOK 3 - BILLY IS NASTY TO ANT

Jealousy only really hurts the person who feels it. It is useful to help children accept other people's successes without them feeling vulnerable. When Ant wins a school prize, Billy can't stop himself saying horrible things. Rather than being pleased for Ant, he is envious and wishes he had won instead.

BOOK 4 - BILLY AND ANT LIE

Lying is very common. It's wrong, but it's common. Lies are told for a number of different reasons, but one of the most frequent is to avoid trouble. While cycling to school, Billy and Ant mess around and lie about getting a flat tyre to cover up their lateness. The arrival of the police at school regarding a serious crime committed earlier that day means their lie puts them in a very difficult position.

BOOK 5 - BILLY HELPS MAX

Stealing is taking something without permission or payment. Children may steal for a dare, or because they want something and have no money, or as a way of getting attention. Stealing shows a lack of self-control. Max sees some go-faster stripes for her bike. She has to have them, but her birthday is ages away. She eventually gives in to temptation.

BOOK 6 - BILLY SAVES THE DAY

Children need belief in themselves and their abilities, but having an inflated ego can be detrimental. Lack of self-belief holds them back, but overpraising leads to unrealistic expectations. Billy fails to audition for the lead role in the school play, as he is convinced he is not good enough.

BOOK 7- BILLY WANTS IT ALL

The value of money is one of the most important subjects for children to learn and carry with them into adulthood, yet it is one of the least-taught subjects. Billy and Ant want skateboards, but soon realise a reasonable one will cost a significant amount of money. How will they get the amount they need?

BOOK 8 – BILLY KNOWS A SECRET

If something has to be kept a secret, there must be a reason. It is usually to protect yourself or someone else. This story explores the issues of secret-keeping by Billy and Ant, and the consequences that arise. For children, the importance of finding a responsible adult with whom they can confide in and share their concerns is a significant life lesson.

ABOUT THE AUTHOR

I am a dad of two grown children, and a stepfather to three more. I started writing five years ago with books designed to appeal to the inner child in adults - very English humour. My daughter Louise, reminded me of the bedtime stories I told her, and suggested I write them down for others to enjoy. I haven't yet, but instead I wrote this eight-book series for 8 to 11-year-olds. These are traditional stories with positive value based plots.

Although the main characters, Billy and his friends, are made up, Billy's dog, Jacko, is based on our much-loved family pet, which, with our second dog Malibu, caused havoc and mayhem to the delight of my children and consternation of me.

Prior to writing, I was a college lecturer, and later worked in the computer industry, at a time before smartphones and tablets, when computers were powered by steam, and stood as high as a bus.

WEBSITES

www.thebillybooks.co.uk

www.jamesminter.com

E-MAIL

james@jamesminter.com

TWITTER

@james_minter

FACEBOOK

facebook.com/thebillybooks/

facebook.com/author.james.minter

ACKNOWLEDGEMENTS

Like all projects of this type, there are always a number of indispensable people who help bring it to completion. They include Christina Lepre, for her editing and incisive comments, suggestions and corrections. Tricia Parker for her proof reading, and Helen Rushworth of Ibex Illustrations, for her images that so capture the mood of the story. Gwen Gades for her cover design. And Maggie, my wife, for putting up with my endless pestering to read, comment and discuss my story, and, through her work as a personal development coach, her editorial input into the learnings designed to help children become responsible adults.

IBEX ILLUSTRATIONS

Printed in Great Britain
by Amazon